MOP TOP

MOP TOP

Story and pictures by Don Freeman

SCHOLASTIC BOOK SERVICES

NEW YORK • LONDON • RICHMOND HILL, ONTARIO

Copyright 1955 by Don Freeman. This edition is published by Scholastic Book Services, a division of Scholastic Magazines, Inc., by arrangement with The Viking Press, Inc.

1st printing .... March 1967

Printed in the U.S.A.

For Chipper and Daryl,
Michael and Diane,
Ethan and Sean,
Jeff and Roy,
and all red-haired topknotters
everywhere

This is the story of a boy
who never wanted to have his hair cut.

Everybody called him Moppy,
because on top he looked like a floppy red mop.

Moppy didn't care what anybody said about his hair
or what they called him.
All he wanted was to stay at home and play.

He sometimes played at being a soaring eagle,

and he sometimes played at being a roaring lion.
A good lion he made, too, without even trying!

But the time came when something had to be done
about Moppy's top. And it happened one day when he
was swinging from branch to branch in his very own
chinaberry tree.

His mother came out into the garden and said,
"Pardon me, but just who do you think you are up
there — Tarzan?"

"Oh no, Mother, I'm not Tarzan!" said Moppy. "I'm a
man from Mars, and I'm visiting all the stars and other
planets!"

"Well then, Mister Man-from-Mars, could you plan to make a landing on this earth sometime today? We want you to hop to the barbershop and get that floppy mop clipped off before your birthday party tomorrow."

The minute Moppy heard the words "birthday party," he dropped down out of the tree to the ground, feet first, then stretched out his hand.

"Here's some money, sonny," his mother said. "I've just called Mister Barberoli, and he says he'll be ready for you at four o'clock sharp. It's a little after half past three now, so let's see you hippity-hop to the barbershop all by yourself."

Moppy put the money in his pocket, and off he
zoomed across the vacant lot, like a rocket to the moon.

But just as soon as he turned the corner,
he slowed down to a trot.

"Don't need my hair cut at all — anyway not now,"
he grumbled, and stumbled along until some bright red
lollipops in a candy-store window caught his eye. They
looked so good he had to stop.

While he stood there staring, what should waddle up
but a frilly woolly pup.

"What a silly-looking pup you are!" said Moppy as he bent down and tried to find the pup's eyes. "You're the one who needs a haircut, not me!"

And then they both trotted away in opposite
directions.

Moppy hadn't gone very far before he saw
Mr. Lawson mowing his lawn.

"That lawn is what needs a haircut, not me!"
said Moppy.

Mr. Lawson stopped to wipe his brow and said,
"How about letting me use this machine on that grassy
patch of yours, boy? It could do with a little mowing."

Moppy thought he ought to get going, so off
he hopped.

But the closer he got to the barbershop,
the slower he hopped.

He was nearly there when he saw a man on a ladder,
snipping branches off a low, droopy tree.

"Maybe a tree needs a clipping, but not me!"
said Moppy.

"Oh, I don't know about that," said the man on the
ladder. "You could do with a few snips of these snippers,
skipper!"

At that, Moppy skipped away
and came at last to the barbershop.

But hard as he tried, he could not go inside!

He decided to run and hide in the grocery store next door, where he could think things over.

And this is where he hid — behind a barrel of brooms
and brushes and fancy red mops!

By and by a lady without her glasses came up and told the salesman she wanted a mop to help her keep her kitchen floor clean.

"What's more, I want the strongest, fluffiest, floppiest mop you have in the store, sir," she said as she began shaking the mops, one at a time.

"Here, this one will do very well," said the lady.
"I'll take it along with me right now."

"Ouch! Let go!" shouted Moppy. "I'm not a mop!
I'm a boy!"

The lady certainly did let go, and in a hurry too,
as Moppy scurried out the door and headed straight for
Mister Barberoli's barbershop!

"I thought maybe you forgot," said roly-poly Mister
Barberoli. "But you're right on the dot. It's exactly four!"
Then in one long leap Moppy was up on the barber-chair
seat ready to get his hair cut nice and neat.

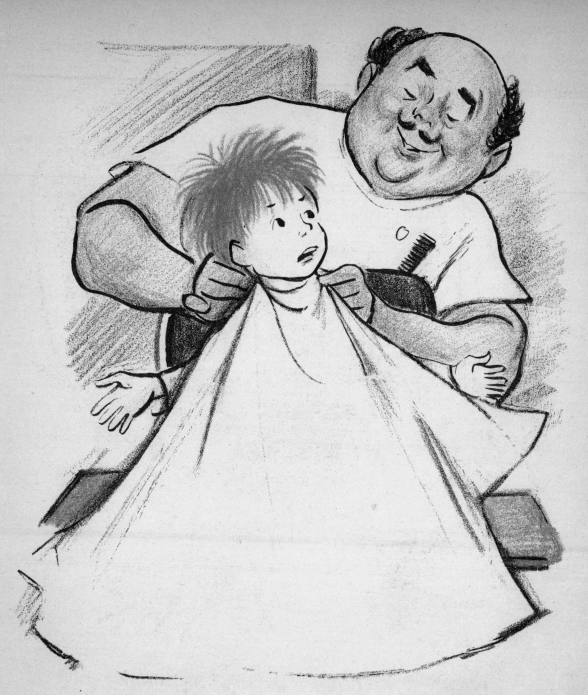

"Please, Mister Barberoli, don't let me look like a
mop any more," pleaded Moppy.
"I don't want to clean anybody's kitchen floor!"

In a jiffy, Mister Barberoli was clipping and snipping away, and combing and cropping without once stopping, as if he hadn't a minute to lose.

Finally he did stop. He held up a mirror and said,
"Well, sonny, who's that, would you say?"

"It's me! It's me without that floppy old mop on top!
Hooray!" said the boy in the chair.

Then he hopped down and gave Mister Barberoli the
money. And out the door he flew, light as a feather.

All the world looked spick-and-span, as the boy who
was once called Moppy hopped up the street for home.

Everything felt new now, even the weather!
The tree was neat and tidy. The lawn was nicely mowed.
And look at the pup! Even he's had a trim!

Next day at his birthday party there was a beautiful
big cake with six candles lit, and on the frosting
was written

HAPPY BIRTHDAY TO MARTY!

which was his real and true name all the time
and forevermore!